This book is dedicated to Dr. Naomi Rose. Her advice and encouragement helped enormously in its writing.
—R.R.

To Peyton
—J.S.G.

Text copyright © 2015 by Ron Roy
Cover art copyright © 2015 by Stephen Gilpin
Interior illustrations copyright © 2015 by John Steven Gurney

Visit us on the Web!
SteppingStonesBooks.com
randomhousekids.com

Educators and librarians, for a variety of teaching tools,
visit us at RHTeachersLibrarians.com

Library of Congress Cataloging-in-Publication Data
Roy, Ron.
Operation orca / by Ron Roy ; illustrated by John Steven Gurney.
pages cm. — (A to Z mysteries. Super edition ; #7)
"A Stepping Stone book."
Summary: "Dink, Josh, and Ruth Rose must solve a mystery when they go whale watching in Alaska." —Provided by publisher.
ISBN 978-0-553-52396-6 (trade) — ISBN 978-0-553-52397-3 (lib. bdg.) — ISBN 978-0-553-52398-0 (ebook)
[1. Mystery and detective stories. 2. Whale watching—Fiction. 3. Poaching—Fiction. 4. Missing persons—Fiction. 5. Alaska—Fiction.]
I. Gurney, John Steven, illustrator. II. Title.
PZ7.R8139Ope 2015 [Fic]—dc23 2014032379

This book has been officially leveled by using the F&P Text Level Gradient™ Leveling System.

Printed in the United States of America
10 9 8 7 6 5 4 3 2 1

Random House Children's Books supports the First Amendment and celebrates the right to read.

DINK, JOSH, AND RUTH ROSE
AREN'T THE ONLY KID DETECTIVES!

WHAT ABOUT YOU?

CAN YOU FIND THE HIDDEN MESSAGE INSIDE THIS BOOK?

There are 26 illustrations in this book, not counting the one on the title page, the map at the beginning, and the picture of the orcas that repeats at the start of many of the chapters. In each of the 26 illustrations, there's a hidden letter. If you can find all the letters, you will spell out a secret message!

If you're stumped, the answer is on the bottom of page 131.

HAPPY DETECTING!

A to Z Mysteries®

SUPER EDITION 7

Operation Orca

by Ron Roy

illustrated by
John Steven Gurney

A STEPPING STONE BOOK™

Random House 🏠 New York

CHAPTER 1

Dink, Josh, and Ruth Rose walked along the boat dock in Juneau, Alaska. The water in the Gulf of Alaska sparkled under the warm summer sun. The kids wore shorts, T-shirts, and sandals.

They were in Alaska with Dink's father, who was there for work. The kids were going on a whale watch.

"How will we know which boat?" Josh asked. "There are so many!"

"It's called the *Jamaica*," Ruth Rose told him. "The name will be on the side of the boat."

"I wonder why it's called that," Josh said. "We're thousands of miles from Jamaica."

"My dad told me the owner was born in Jamaica," Dink said. "His name is Rafe Johnson, and his boat is painted blue."

"I see about ten blue boats," Josh said. "Navy blue, royal blue, light blue, sky blue, the color blue Ruth Rose is wearing . . ."

Ruth Rose liked to dress all in one color. Today's color was blueberry blue, the same as her eyes.

"Look, there it is!" Ruth Rose yelled.

They ran along the dock, their sandals slapping the wood. The *Jamaica* was bright blue, like the tail feathers on a parrot Dink had seen in Mrs. Wong's pet shop, back in Green Lawn.

The boat was longer than a school bus. Dink noticed an awning where people could sit on deck out of the sun.

JAMAICA had been painted in yellow on one side.

On the dock was a sign:

WHALE-WATCHING CRUISES

SEE ORCAS AND HUMPBACKS!

CONTACT RAFE JOHNSON

RAFEJOHNSON@RAFETHEWHALEMAN.COM

"This is so cool!" Josh said. "I've never seen a whale face to face!"

"Can I help you kiddos?" a voice asked.

The kids whipped around. A tall man stood there, carrying white plastic bags filled with groceries. He wore baggy shorts and a blue T-shirt with I LOVE JAMAICA printed on the front. His long dreadlocks were tied back with a string.

The man smiled. "Oh, wait, are you the ones from Green-something, Connecticut?" he asked.

"Green Lawn," Dink said. "I'm Dink, and these are my friends Josh and Ruth Rose."

"I'm Rafe," the tall man said. He hoisted his bags. "Sorry, can't shake hands."

"Can we carry some for you?" Ruth Rose asked.

"Awesome," Rafe said. He passed the bags to the kids. "You're a day early, aren't you? We're going out tomorrow, right?"

WHALE-WATCHIN
CRUISES

"We landed at the airport a couple of hours ago," Ruth Rose explained. "We're staying at the Turner Hotel." She pointed toward a building not far from the dock.

"We were just exploring and thought we'd check out your boat," Dink added.

"I'm glad you did," Rafe said. "My boat group for today cancelled, so I went grocery shopping. Want to come aboard while I put away this food?"

"Excellent!" Josh said.

JAMAICA

"Mind your feet," Rafe said as he and the kids stepped aboard the *Jamaica*. "If you fall in, the water is pretty cold!"

Josh looked down at the water. "Are there sharks?"

Rafe grinned and nodded. "Yeah, man, there is everything in these waters," he said.

Once aboard, the kids followed Rafe down some stairs into a cabin. Dink looked around. He saw a small table, benches, a kitchen, and shelves of books. He noticed a tiny bathroom, a bed, and a TV.

"This is amazing," Dink said. "You could live here!"

"I do, most of the time," Rafe said. "I also have an apartment in town."

He began pulling food from the bags. "Want to help?" he asked.

"Sure," Dink said for all of them.

"Milk and juice in the fridge, soups

in the cupboard, rice and cereal on the shelf," Rafe told the kids.

When everything was put away, they sat in the shade under the awning. "So are you excited about seeing whales up close?" Rafe asked the kids.

"I couldn't sleep last night!" Ruth Rose said. She showed Rafe her camera. "I'm going to get a zillion pictures!"

"You're lucky to have the chance," Rafe said.

"We got some reward money last year," Josh said. He told Rafe how they had gone to London, England, and found the queen's stolen jewels. "The money is for college, but our parents let us spend some for this trip."

"So where is your dad?" Rafe asked Dink.

"At the hotel," Dink said. "He has a meeting later this afternoon. We have to be back by five."

Rafe looked at his watch. "Here's an idea: Why don't we go out to see a few orcas right now? I know a small pod that isn't too far away. I'd have you back here in a few hours."

"Cool!" Dink said. "Let me call my dad."

Dink pulled a cell phone from his pocket and called his father. They had a short conversation, and Dink grinned. "My dad said it's fine—just don't fall overboard!"

Rafe laughed. "You're safe with Rafe," he said. "While I get us under way, you three put on life vests, please. They're in the aft storage locker."

"The *what* storage locker?" Josh asked.

"Aft," Rafe said. He pointed to the rear of the boat. "Back there is *aft.*" Then he pointed to the front of the boat. "The front is *fore*. Fore and aft, front and back."

The kids walked aft, found the

locker, and pulled on the orange vests. They heard the *Jamaica*'s engine roar to life, and a few minutes later they were headed out to sea.

CHAPTER 2

After about thirty minutes, Rafe slowed the *Jamaica*. The boat settled in the water with its engine idling quietly. The sea was calm, and the kids could hear seagull cries over the boat's motor. Rafe swept his binoculars across the water, turning in a circle.

"I don't see any whales," Josh said, peering down into the water.

"This is the right area," Rafe said quietly. "Maybe not the exact spot. Orcas move around, following the fish they want to eat."

Ruth Rose had pulled her binoculars from her backpack.

"Look for a white splash or a tall black fin," Rafe said. "When orcas come to the surface, they exhale, and that sends warm breath and water into the cooler air. It's like steam, but from a distance we see a little splash."

Rafe's boat made a big, slow circle. He held binoculars up to his eyes as he steered with the other hand. "There, to the left!" he said after a few minutes.

The kids looked. A hundred yards away, they saw several splashes and black fins as orcas surfaced.

"Oh my gosh!" Josh yelled. "I'm actually looking at whales!"

"Technically, you're looking at dolphins," Rafe said. "Orcas are the largest members of the dolphin family."

"Are they playing?" Josh asked.

"They might be," Rafe said. "But they

have to come to the surface to breathe every few minutes. That's when we get to see their dorsal fins, the tall ones on their backs."

Rafe took the *Jamaica* a little closer to the action. Now the kids could see the small geysers of air mixed with water made by the orcas when they breathed out.

"All whales breathe through blow-holes on the top of their heads," Rafe said. "Some whales have two holes, but orcas have just one. When they hit the surface, they blow out to get rid of old air. Then they take in more oxygen quickly before they dive again."

Suddenly a large orca shot out of the water. The black-and-white body gleamed under the sun before the orca landed back in the water, making a huge splash.

"Oh my gosh!" Ruth Rose cried.

"That's so cool! Why did it do that?"

"That's called breaching," Rafe said. "Most kinds of whales breach. Some sharks do, too."

"But why do they do it?" Dink asked.

"Scientists aren't one hundred percent sure," Rafe said. "But most think breaching helps the animals get rid of barnacles and lice that live on their bodies. When they hit the water, the little things get knocked off."

Rafe grinned. "Other scientists think orcas breach just for fun, the way we humans play in our swimming pools."

"Look, what's that one doing?" Dink asked. He pointed to an orca with the top half of its body out of the water. "He looks like he's watching us!"

"That's exactly what he's doing," Rafe said. "When they sit half out of the water like that, it's called spy-hopping. He's spying on my boat!"

"You're teasing us, right?" Josh asked.

"Nope, not teasing," Rafe said. "Orcas are smart and curious. They know the boat is here, but they can't see all of it from under the water. So they raise the top part of their body out of the water, and then they can see what's on the surface."

"But how do they do it?" Dink asked.

"They use their tails for balance, and their pectoral fins—their side fins— to stay upright," Rafe explained. "We do the same thing with our legs and arms when we tread water."

"That is so cool!" Josh said. "We're watching them, and they're watching us!"

The kids laughed as another orca popped up next to the first one that was spy-hopping.

Suddenly a tall black fin rose much closer to the boat. The orca exhaled, making a whooshing sound and creating a plume of air and water.

"Look at his dorsal fin!" Rafe said. "See where it looks like it got bitten? Probably fighting another orca. This is the biggest male in the pod. I call him Jack."

The orca disappeared as quickly as he had appeared.

"Jack will be back," Rafe said.

"How do you know he's a male?" Ruth Rose asked.

"His dorsal fin points straight up," Rafe answered. "Females and young orcas have curved dorsal fins."

The kids watched as other orcas rose, breathed, then sank away again. They tried to identify males and females. Jack surfaced every few minutes, and he didn't seem afraid of the boat.

They could easily see the nick in his dorsal fin.

"Look," Rafe said in a low voice. "See the curved dorsal fin on that female? I call her Lily. She has a tear in her fin just above her back. Something bit her there."

"Why did you name her Lily?" Dink asked.

Rafe grinned. "That's my mother's name," he said. "And Lily has a baby, but I don't see it yet. The baby's dorsal fin will be much smaller."

"Did you name the baby Rafe?" Josh asked, grinning.

Rafe laughed. "No," he said. "I don't know whether it's a male or female. We'll have to wait till it's older."

The kids watched for Lily each time the orcas rose for air. Rafe had his binoculars ready. "There, on her right side!" he said suddenly. "That's the calf!"

The kids saw a small plume of air and water, and a much smaller dorsal fin. The little orca swam next to Lily, so close that their bodies touched. The mother was about three times as long as her calf.

"How big is the baby?" asked Ruth Rose. She had her binoculars trained on the mother and calf.

"Well, Lily is about twenty feet long—half the length of my boat. I'd guess she weighs around seven thousand pounds," Rafe said. "Her baby is maybe seven or eight feet, around three hundred pounds."

"Why does the baby's skin look kind of orange in the white parts?" Josh asked.

"The skin is white, but what you're seeing is the blood vessels *under* the skin," Rafe explained. "Young orcas have thin skin, but as they grow older, they get more fat and we can't see the blood vessels. In a year or so, the calf will look black and white, like Lily."

"It wants to play!" Josh said, pointing. The young orca was bumping Lily in her side.

"The calf wants to suckle," Rafe said. "There are slits on the mother's side, and that's where the babies get their milk. This one will nurse from Lily for a year or two before it stops."

"What do adult orcas eat?" Dink asked Rafe.

"Orcas are carnivores," Rafe said. "Some eat mostly fish, like herring and salmon, even sharks. Other orcas seem to prefer seals and other sea creatures. Sometimes they go after whales."

"Do they ever eat humans?" Josh asked.

Rafe shook his head. "Orcas in the wild have never been known to attack people," he said.

"Good!" said Josh.

Rafe fired up his engine and started back toward town. The kids sat under the awning drinking lemonade.

Josh pointed to something out in the distance. "Look at that huge boat!" he said.

"That's the *Miranda*," Rafe said, peering through his binoculars. "It's owned by Drake Turner. He lives down in Ketchikan, Alaska, about two hundred miles southeast of here."

"It looks pretty big," Josh said.

"Yep, about three times the size of the *Jamaica*," Rafe said.

Dink did the math. "The *Miranda* is one hundred twenty feet long!"

"Why does Mr. Turner call it the *Miranda*?" asked Dink.

"He named the boat after his wife," Rafe said.

The *Miranda* was going slowly, and soon Rafe had left the big yacht in his wake.

CHAPTER 3

They were back at the boat harbor before five o'clock. The sun was just beginning to cast shadows along the wooden dock.

Dink, Josh, and Ruth Rose thanked Rafe. "What time should we be here tomorrow morning with my dad?" Dink asked him.

"How about ten o'clock?" Rafe asked. "I'll pack lunch, and we'll spend a whole day looking at orcas and humpbacks."

The kids waved good-bye and headed for the hotel. They passed a lot of other boats as they walked along the dock. Some were sailboats with tall masts. Others were working boats, like Rafe's. The kids saw people on some of the boat decks. Others seemed empty.

Most of the boats had names painted on their sides. One was called *Dad's Hobby.* Another read *Gone Fishing.*

Suddenly they heard an engine roar to life. A few yards away, one of the boats backed out of its slip. It was about the same length as the *Jamaica,* with an awning covering part of the deck. Behind the awning Dink noticed a machine. It had an arm, like a small crane. Long fishing rods were mounted to a wall.

"Everyone else is coming in," Dink said. "I wonder why that boat is going out."

"Maybe they're going fishing," Josh said.

As the boat backed away, Dink noticed the name on the side: NOT MY FALT.

"*Fault* isn't spelled right," Ruth Rose said.

As they entered the hotel lobby, a man wearing green shorts and a white shirt was just leaving. He carried a brief-case in one hand. The initials *D.T.* were stamped into the leather.

As the man passed him, Dink noticed words on the back of his shirt: COOL POOL BROTHERS.

The man hurried down the steps and got into a white van parked out

front. COOL POOL BROTHERS was painted on it. Under the words was a picture of children splashing in a swimming pool.

Dink watched the man pull away into traffic. "Did that guy look familiar to you?" he asked Josh and Ruth Rose.

"Nope," Josh said.

Chester, the hotel manager, was in his office sitting at a desk. A TV was showing a soccer game. The office also held a sofa and a small fridge.

As they approached the counter, Dink saw Chester open the desk's drawer and drop something inside. To Dink, it looked like a stack of money.

"Hi, Chester," Ruth Rose said.

Chester locked the drawer, put the key in his pocket, and walked over to the counter. "Welcome back," he said. "Did you find Rafe Johnson okay?"

"Yes, and he took us out to see some orcas!" Josh said.

"We saw a baby one!" Dink said.

"We're going back out tomorrow," Ruth Rose said.

"Great," Chester said. "Rafe really knows a lot about whales."

Just then a stranger brushed past the kids at the counter. He was tall and wore khakis, a pressed shirt, and sunglasses. The man stuck his hand out over the counter. "Any mail for me, Chester?" he asked quietly.

Chester smiled at the man. "Hi, Mr. Turner. I wasn't expecting you for a couple of weeks," he said. Chester handed him an envelope.

The man studied the envelope, then sighed and walked toward the elevator.

"How long will you be staying, sir?" Chester asked. But he didn't get an answer. The elevator doors opened, and the stranger stepped inside.

"Who was that?" Ruth Rose asked. "He seemed kind of sad."

"That's Mr. Drake Turner," Chester said. "He owns this hotel." Chester shook his head. "He's sad a lot."

"Hey, we saw his yacht when we were on Rafe's boat!" Josh said.

"Yes, the *Miranda*," Chester said. "He often motors it up here, but sometimes he brings his helicopter instead."

"He has a helicopter *and* a yacht?" Josh said with wide eyes. "He must be pretty rich!"

"Rich indeed," Chester said. "He also owns a mansion on an island in Ketchikan. He built his own saltwater pond there, and he keeps it filled with fish and other sea creatures. I hear he has seals and dolphins."

Chester pointed up toward the ceiling. "You should see his penthouse on the top floor," he added.

"Wow, does he land his helicopter on the roof?" Josh asked.

Chester shook his head. "No, he owns

some land behind the town library," he said. "That's where his pilot sets the chopper whenever Mr. Turner wants to stay in his penthouse."

"Why doesn't he just sleep on his boat?" Dink asked.

Chester leaned closer to the kids. "I think he keeps the apartment upstairs because it reminds him of his wife and son," he said. "That's the last place he saw them before they disappeared."

Josh gulped. "Disappeared?"

Chester nodded. "Gone," he said.

Dink, Josh, and Ruth Rose stared at Chester. "Did they die?" Ruth Rose whispered.

Chester shook his head. "No, they just walked out," he said. "It happened about a year ago. While Mr. Turner was at a meeting, his wife took the boy and left. Mr. Turner hasn't seen them since. He keeps expecting a letter, but it never comes."

"That *is* pretty sad," Dink said.

"How old is his son?" Ruth Rose asked.

"Tyler was five when they left," Chester said. "A real cute kid—hair as red as yours, Josh. Mr. Turner misses them terribly."

"Why doesn't he just ask them to come back?" Ruth Rose asked.

Chester picked up a brass nameplate that read: CHESTER TOOMEY, MGR. He gave it a quick polish with his sleeve and set it back on the counter.

Finally, Chester looked at the kids. "Mr. Turner doesn't know where they are," he said. "His wife left a note telling him not to look for them, but he does anyway. He hired the best detective agency in Alaska. The detectives searched everywhere, but no luck."

"But doesn't Tyler want to see his dad?" Josh asked. "Doesn't he miss him?"

"I don't know," Chester said. "But I sure do miss that little kid. The other staff here miss him, too. Mr. Turner never spent much time with Tyler. So we used to read to him all the time, and play games with him."

Chester smiled. "Tyler had a favorite book he carried around with him. It was called *Wonderful Island.* He'd beg us to read it to him, sometimes two or three times a day. I must have read that book to Tyler a hundred times."

"Why did Tyler and his mom leave?" Ruth Rose asked.

Chester looked sad. "Mr. Turner spent so much time making deals and money that he had no time for his family," he said. "I guess his wife got sick of it. So she took Tyler and left."

CHAPTER 4

The kids got in the elevator. Their rooms were on the third floor. It was a small hotel, with just a few rooms on each floor.

"Look," Josh said inside the elevator. His finger was an inch from a button with 4-P printed on it. "I'll bet *P* stands for *penthouse*, and it's right above our floor!"

"Don't even think about pushing that button," Dink said, pressing the button for the third floor.

He and Josh shared a room, next to Ruth Rose's. Dink's father's room was across the hall.

Josh used the key card, and the three kids piled into the boys' room.

Dink ran over and pulled the drapes, revealing sliding glass doors and a balcony.

Josh yanked the doors open, and the room filled with cool air that smelled like the ocean. The kids stepped onto the balcony, shielding their eyes against the sun. Seagulls soared and screamed over the water.

"Look, there's the *Jamaica*!" Josh said.

Ruth Rose got out her binoculars. "I can see Rafe!" she said.

The kids all yelled and waved, but the *Jamaica* was too far away for Rafe to hear them.

Ruth Rose swept the binoculars across the harbor. "A lot of people are cooking and eating on their boats," she said.

"Can you see Mr. Turner's yacht?" Josh asked.

Ruth Rose moved the binoculars to the right. "Yup, it's way out, tied to one of those buoy things," she said. "It must be too big to tie up at the dock like Rafe's boat."

"When I become a billionaire, I'll buy a humongous boat," Josh said. "I'll grow a beard and wear a captain's hat."

"Can we be your crew?" Dink said.

Josh grinned. "Yeah, you can cook all my meals. Ice cream every day!"

The kids showered and changed, and went out for pizza with Dink's father.

That night, Dink dreamed he was back on a boat. It was longer and newer than the *Jamaica.* Josh was the captain, and they were going to look for whales. When they found a pod of orcas, Captain Josh stopped the boat.

Suddenly the orcas rose out of the water, spy-hopping. They all started making noises and waving their fins.

"What are you trying to tell me?" Dink asked the orcas. He finally woke up with his sheet and blankets twisted around his body.

Later, Dink told Josh and Ruth Rose about his dream. "They were making squeaky noises," Dink said. "I wish I could speak orca."

After breakfast, the kids walked down to the boat dock with Dink's father. They all wore baseball caps, and they had smeared sunblock on their arms, necks, and faces. Dink's father wore sunglasses and a New York Yankees cap.

Rafe waved as they approached the *Jamaica.* "Right on time," he said, shaking hands with Dink's father. "You and Dink look a lot alike!"

Dink showed his dad where the life

vests were kept, and they all chose one and put it on. The four of them sat under the awning and watched Rafe back the *Jamaica* out of its slip.

The engine was loud, so no one spoke. Rafe expertly took his boat over the waves without making too many big splashes.

Dink and Josh stared over the side, hoping to see whales or sharks or dolphins.

Ruth Rose was looking through her binoculars.

"See anything interesting?" Dink's father asked.

She told him about the *Miranda*, Drake Turner's big yacht. "It's tied up right over there."

"May I see?" he asked.

Ruth Rose handed him the binoculars.

"Mmm, nice," Dink's father said when he had located the *Miranda* at its mooring. "Someone is looking back at

us." He handed the binoculars to Ruth Rose.

Suddenly the *Jamaica* slowed and settled in the water. Rafe cut the engine to a low purr. "We're here," he said. He held his binoculars up to his eyes.

Josh looked around at the miles of ocean. "How can you tell we're in the right spot?" he asked.

"The pod will be spread out over a range," Rafe said. "But remember, they follow the fish or whatever they're after."

After a few minutes, Rafe moved the boat to another spot several hundred yards away, cruising slowly. He saw no fins or spouts of water and air, so he moved the *Jamaica* again.

"It's so quiet," Dink said.

Then, just to prove him wrong, a group of seagulls flew low over the boat, screeching.

"Good sign," Rafe said. "That means there are fish nearby."

"I think I see a fin!" Ruth Rose said suddenly. "Over there!" She pointed while looking through her binoculars.

"Good eye, Ruth Rose!" Josh said.

Rafe moved the boat a little closer. Then he powered down, and the *Jamaica* sat quietly in the water. About a hundred yards away, they all saw waterspouts and black fins.

"I see Jack!" Rafe said. "It's the same pod." After a minute, he added, "They're acting strange. They seem to be just swimming around, not really doing anything."

"Can you see Lily and her baby?" Dink asked.

"Can't tell," Rafe said. "I see females, but I can't spot the nick in her dorsal fin from here."

They all watched quietly, looking especially for Lily and her calf.

CHAPTER 5

"Could Lily just be somewhere else today?" Ruth Rose asked.

Rafe shook his head. "She wouldn't go off alone. Members of pods are family," he said. "Lily stays with the pod, and her calf would never leave her."

Then Rafe put a finger to his lips. "Listen," he said. "You can hear the orcas' cries right through the bottom of my boat."

The kids got down on the deck and put their ears to the wood.

"I hear them!" Josh said. "It sounds like they're calling to each other."

Rafe got down lower and listened. "Something isn't right here," he said. "The orcas are acting odd, and their underwater cries don't sound normal, either."

"Is that Lily?" Dink's father asked, pointing to a fin several yards from the boat. "You said she had a scar on her dorsal fin."

Rafe looked. "Yep, that's Lily. But I don't see the calf," he said.

Lily took in some air through her blowhole. Then her fin disappeared.

They all watched for Lily to surface again. She did, every few minutes. But no one saw the calf.

"Do you think something bad happened?" Josh asked.

Rafe nodded, still staring at the water. "Yes, I think something very bad happened," he said.

Rafe stepped into his cabin. Dink, Josh, Ruth Rose, and Dink's father

kept their eyes on the water. Seagulls screeched and the boat's engine hummed. Even with these sounds, the kids could still hear orca cries through the hull of the boat.

Lily surfaced again, and she was alone. Other orcas were nearby, but the kids saw no calf.

They told Rafe when he came out of his cabin. He was carrying a small wooden box.

"That's what I was afraid of," Rafe said, opening the box. "I think Lily has

lost her baby, and she's grieving."

"Lost it?" Dink asked. "What do you mean?"

"The baby might have died," Rafe said. "Or it might have been taken by poachers."

The kids and Dink's father stared at Rafe.

"It doesn't happen often, but sometimes baby whales get stolen and sold," he said.

"How old is the calf?" Dink's father asked.

"About three months," Rafe said. "Still getting milk from Lily, which is why I'm really concerned. A young orca needs its mother's milk for at least a year, sometimes longer."

From the box, Rafe took a silvery object attached to a long cable. He made a few adjustments, flicked a switch, and lowered the device and its cable over the side of the boat. He set the box on the deck and turned a few knobs.

"What's that?" Josh asked.

"It's called a hydrophone," Rafe said. "Really just an underwater microphone."

After a minute, they all heard strange, eerie sounds coming from speakers above them. The same noises could be faintly heard through the boat's hull.

They heard a long cry. It went on and on.

"That sounds . . . sad," Dink whispered.

"That's Lily crying out for her calf," Rafe said.

The underwater noises went on for a minute or two, then faded away. Finally, all the sounds stopped. "I guess the pod left the area," Rafe said.

"But what happened to the baby?" Ruth Rose asked.

"Did a shark get it?" Josh asked.

"I doubt it," Rafe said. "It's very rare for a baby orca to be killed by a predator. Orcas are fierce fighters, and the pod would fight off any shark."

"Then someone really did take it?" Dink asked.

Rafe pulled the hydrophone out of the water, coiled the cable, and returned the device to the box. "I think so," he said.

"But isn't that illegal?" Dink's father asked.

"It sure is," Rafe said. "The U.S. has strict laws about taking marine mammals of any kind. It's also illegal to feed or touch them. The government almost never allows anyone to take a young whale out of these waters. If someone took Lily's calf, they're breaking the law."

"But how do all those theme parks get whales and dolphins and stuff?" Josh asked. "Like you see on TV?"

Rafe shrugged. "Most of them do it the proper way," he said. "They get an official permit from a government agency. But there are always a few bad guys who break the law. They wait till the middle of the night, when no other boats are around. They come out here, take a baby whale, then go back to shore. A poacher can sell a young whale or dolphin for a lot of money."

"How do they catch the baby?" Ruth Rose asked.

"They need a big boat and nets," Rafe said. "First they find a pod that has a baby with its mother. The guys on the boat surround the pod with a long net, so the whales can't swim away. Then they go after the baby. When the mother and calf come up for air, they drop a small net around the little one. They haul it aboard, bring it to shore, and take the poor thing away to sell."

Rafe shook his head. "The mother calls for her baby, and the little one calls back at her," he said. "What we heard before was all the whales crying out for the missing calf."

"But how do the bad guys take the whale away on land?" Dink asked.

"This calf could easily be hauled off in a small truck," Rafe said.

"Doesn't it need water?" Ruth Rose asked.

"Sure," Rafe said. "The poachers would keep it wet. Sometimes they put the calves in tanks of water. A whale would be okay for several hours that way."

"But that's . . . that's so cruel!" Ruth Rose said.

"Worse than cruel," Rafe told the group. "Lily's calf—if it *has* been taken by poachers—will starve to death in a day or two without her milk."

"That is so disgusting!" Josh said.

"You call it disgusting," Rafe said. "I call it murder."

CHAPTER 6

"Listen to this," Rafe said. He pulled a small tape recorder from the box and inserted a tape.

"A friend sent me this," Rafe told them. "He's really into whales, like me."

He turned up the volume and they all heard a loud crying noise. The crying went on and on.

"That sounds just like Lily did!" Ruth Rose said.

Rafe nodded. "You're listening to another mother orca. My friend named her Naomi," he said. "Naomi's part of a pod south of here. Her baby drowned in a net, and she's grieving. My friend caught the sounds off his boat with his hydrophone."

They all listened to the awful cries coming from the recorder. Dink got goose bumps on his arms.

"Can Naomi have another baby?" Ruth Rose asked.

"If she's young enough, she might," Rafe said, turning off the recorder. "Usually females wait three to five years between one birth and the next."

"What about Lily?" Dink asked.

"Sure, she might have another calf in a few years," Rafe said, powering up his boat. "We've done all we can for now. Ready to see some more whales?"

As the *Jamaica* cruised slowly away, Dink kept his eyes on the water. He had his fingers crossed, hoping to spot Lily and her calf. He didn't see them.

At four in the afternoon, Rafe pulled the *Jamaica* into its slip at the dock. Dink's father and the kids were hot, tired, and a little sunburned. They all thanked Rafe as they climbed off his boat.

As they walked toward the end of the dock, Dink noticed the Cool Pool Brothers van parked near a shady tree. The man he'd seen leaving the hotel was leaning against the van with binoculars up to his eyes.

As the kids passed the van, the man said, "The boat won't be here with the catch till midnight, so get comfortable. We're going to be here awhile."

Another man was opening the van's rear doors. "They'd better show up with the goods," he said. "Those big nets we gave them were expensive!"

Dink turned around and looked into the back of the van. He saw a long tank half-filled with water.

Dink stopped, staring at the van. Thoughts buzzed around in his brain like angry wasps.

He felt his dad's hand on his shoulder. "You okay, bud? Did you get too much sun today?"

"No, I'm fine, Dad," Dink said. "In fact, why don't you go back to the hotel without us? We're going to hang out down here for a while."

"We are?" Josh said. "I need a shower!"

Dink grabbed Josh's arm and gave him a look. "Come on, Josh and Ruth Rose, let's go check out some of those boats. See you later, Dad."

Dink's father waved, then headed up the dock. Dink pulled Josh and Ruth Rose over to a bench.

"What's going on?" Ruth Rose asked.

"Shhh," Dink said. He pointed at the
Cool Pool Brothers van.

"What about it?" Josh asked.

"Keep your voice down," Dink said.
"That van and one of those guys were
at the hotel before. And I just heard the
other one say something about buying
nets. They're waiting for a boat to come
in at midnight! With a catch!"

Josh and Ruth Rose just looked at
Dink.

"And," Dink went on, lowering his voice even more, "there's a tank of water in the back of their van!"

"So they have water in their van," Josh said. He grinned at Dink. "They're *pool* guys, dude."

"Wait, let me finish," Dink said. "Remember Rafe told us how you'd need a boat and nets to steal a baby whale? What if the boat these guys are waiting for has Lily's baby? What if they're going to bring the baby here at midnight? And what if those Cool Pool guys are going to take it away in their van?"

Josh stood up to get a better look at the van.

"Don't stare!" Dink hissed, pulling Josh back onto the bench. Dink pointed at the man holding the binoculars. "That guy was carrying a briefcase when he came out of the hotel. When we got inside, I saw Chester put something in a drawer, real fast. I'm pretty sure it was money!"

Suddenly Dink slapped his forehead. "I forgot something!" he said. "The brief-case had initials on it. *D.T.*"

"Maybe Chester and those pool guys are in it together!" Josh said. "A whale-stealing gang! Maybe Chester's job is finding someone with enough money to buy a baby whale. He works in a hotel, so he'd meet plenty of rich people."

"Oh my gosh!" Ruth Rose said. "Drake Turner is rich, and his initials are D.T. If the pool guy had *his* briefcase, that would mean Drake Turner is part of the gang!"

CHAPTER 7

"Why would the pool guy have Drake Turner's briefcase?" Josh asked.

"Maybe Mr. Turner gave the pool guy the money to give to Chester," Ruth Rose said. "You know, paying him off."

"That doesn't make sense," Josh said. "Mr. Turner could pay Chester himself anytime he wanted just by coming down the elevator. Why have the pool guy do it?"

Dink thought for a minute. "Okay, how's this: What if Mr. Turner wants to buy a baby whale for his private pond? He knows it's illegal. So he gets Chester to work out the deal. Chester hires the pool guys to find someone with a boat who can steal the baby whale. Then Mr. Turner gives the pool guys a briefcase full of money to pay Chester and the guys on the boat."

"It still doesn't make sense," Josh said. "If Mr. Turner got Chester to find the pool guys and hire them, Chester would be paying them; they wouldn't be paying him."

The three kids sat for a minute, thinking about Drake Turner paying to have someone kidnap Lily's baby.

"Okay, so if the boat comes at midnight, and the pool guys put the baby whale in their van," Josh asked, "what do they do with it next?"

"I thought about that, too," Dink said. "The fastest way to get the baby orca out of here is by helicopter, and Mr. Drake Turner just happens to own one! So after the pool guys get the whale, either they or Chester pay off the boat guys. Then they take the calf to Mr. Turner at his helicopter pad behind the library. They load the calf, and the chopper flies away. They do it all at midnight, when no one is around."

"Chester said he wasn't expecting Drake Turner for another two weeks," Josh added. "He must have come sooner because he knew Chester's guys captured the baby orca!"

"We need to spy on Mr. Turner," Ruth Rose said. "He's probably up in his penthouse waiting to hear from the Cool Pool guys that they have the calf. If his helicopter lands, the baby orca will disappear forever."

"I think we should call the police now," Josh said. "If we tell them the plan, they can surround the helicopter when it lands!"

"Josh, we can't prove any of this,"
Dink said. "We can't ask the police to
wait for a helicopter that might not even
land."

"So what *should* we do?" Josh asked.
"That baby orca will die without Lily!"

"I think it would be smarter to keep
an eye on those pool guys," Dink said.
He nodded toward the van. "If I'm right,
we'll see them putting the baby in the
van. Then we call the police before they
take it to the helicopter!"

"It's four in the afternoon," Josh said.
"You said the boat is supposed to come
around midnight, right?"

Dink nodded. "That's what I heard
one of them say."

"So do we just sit here all afternoon
watching two guys who are waiting for a
boat?" Josh looked at his watch. "That's
eight hours!"

"We can leave and come back later,"

Ruth Rose said. "We'll hide somewhere and wait for the boat to come in."

"My dad will never let us come down here tonight," Dink said. Then he grinned. "I guess I could tell him we were all sleepwalking."

"Your dad would be proud of us if we saved that baby whale," Josh said.

Dink nodded. "Let's go back to the hotel," he said. "After my dad goes to bed, we can . . . wait, how do we get past Chester or whoever is at the desk later tonight?"

Ruth Rose grinned. "Chester is on duty until morning," she said. "I happened to peek at his calendar. I bet he'll be sleeping or watching TV. We'll creep past the counter. He'll never see us!"

Josh put up his hand for a high five. "That's an awesome plan, Ruth Rose Hathaway," he said. "I love it when you get all sneaky!"

The kids left the harbor. "Why don't

we try to find Mr. Turner's helicopter pad?" Dink suggested. "His chopper could already be there, waiting."

"It's behind the library," Ruth Rose said. "But we don't know where that is."

"Easy peasy," Josh said. He walked up to a man with a black poodle on a leash. "Excuse me. Can you tell us where the town library is?"

The man smiled and pointed along Main Street. "Juneau has three libraries, but the closest one is right up the street, past the Ho-Ho Doughnut Shop," he said.

"Thank you!" Josh said.

The kids crossed the street and walked until they stood in front of a tiny brick building. JUNEAU PUBLIC LIBRARY was carved into the concrete over the entrance. A woman stood on the steps, washing the glass doors.

She noticed the kids and dropped her cleaning cloth into a bucket. "Hello there," she said, looking them over. "Do I know you?"

"We're from Connecticut," Dink said. "I'm Dink, and these are my friends Josh and Ruth Rose."

"Pleased to meet you," the woman said. "I'm Carol Waxman, the librarian."

"Is the library open?" Ruth Rose asked.

"Oh yes—would you like to come in?" Carol asked. "I'm afraid you can't take any books out since you don't live here, but you can browse all you want!"

Carol held the door open, and the kids walked in. Books were piled everywhere. Not just on the shelves, but on tables and chairs, even stacked high on the floor and jammed tight on the windowsills.

A man sat in a corner with a pile of newspapers on his lap, reading. Two teenage girls sat at a table, looking at magazines and whispering.

"Please don't mind the mess," Carol told Dink, Josh, and Ruth Rose. "We ran out of book space years ago. The other two libraries in town are crammed, too. I stick books wherever I can find a spot. But don't worry—I can find any book in the building!"

"Can we just walk around?" Dink asked.

"Of course," Carol said. "If you see something you like, plop down somewhere and read to your heart's content!"

Dink headed for the rear of the library. He found a window and looked out. He saw a grassy field with a circle painted in black. "That's it," he mumbled.

"What's it?" Josh asked. He and Ruth Rose had walked up behind him.

"Drake Turner lands his helicopter right there," Dink said.

"Fingers crossed it doesn't land there tonight," Ruth Rose said. She crossed her fingers.

CHAPTER 8

The kids walked through the children's section of the library. Everywhere they looked, they saw stacks of books, boxes of books, bags of books. The shelves were packed with books, so tightly Dink figured it would be impossible to pull one out.

Josh bumped into a stack, nearly knocking it over. "They need a bigger library," he muttered. "How are you supposed to find the book you want?"

Josh's question gave Dink an idea. He turned toward Carol Waxman's desk.

"Excuse me. Do you have a book called *Wonderful Island*?" he asked.

Carol closed her eyes. "Sounds familiar," she said. "Do you know the author?"

"No, sorry," Dink said.

"Is it a children's book?" Carol asked.

Dink nodded. "For little kids, I think," he said. "We know a five-year-old boy who read it over and over."

"Oh, a five-year-old? That makes finding it simpler," Carol said. "Give me a few minutes."

The librarian disappeared around a corner. The kids heard her moving books and muttering to herself. Then they heard "Aha! Found you!"

Carol came back to the desk carrying a thin picture book.

"*Wonderful Island* by Jamie Cooper," she said, holding the book out to Dink. "Now I remember! A few years ago I read this to a group of kindergartners. As I recall, they adored it!"

Dink, Josh, and Ruth Rose sat at a table and read the book. There were lots of pictures and not many words. The story was about Jamie Cooper when he was a boy. One summer, his parents rented a house on an island in a lake in Maine. The kids read about how Jamie learned to swim and sail a boat. He learned how to read animal tracks in the dirt around his house. He found an orphan bunny and fed it milk from a baby bottle. He picked blueberries and fed them to the ducks and chipmunks.

"Wow, that Jamie was a lucky kid," Josh said.

Ruth Rose read the front flap of the book jacket. "This is a true story," she said.

Josh asked, "So is this island a real place?"

Ruth Rose turned to the back of the book and read aloud: *"As a boy, author Jamie Cooper spent many happy summers on Sebago Lake and Frye Island with his family. Now that he is grown, Mr. Cooper brings his own family back to Frye Island every summer."*

"There's a picture of Frye Island," Josh said. "It's shaped like a whale."

"That's so cool!" Ruth Rose said. "Look, that little beach area looks like the whale's mouth!"

They returned *Wonderful Island* to Carol and thanked her. She had an armful of books, trying to find room on a shelf. "You're entirely welcome," she said. Then she sighed. "Now if I just had a few more rooms for all these books, I'd be a happy woman!"

"Why doesn't the town build a bigger library?" Josh asked.

"Money, honey," Carol said, letting out a big sigh. "If I ever win the lottery, I'll expand this library myself. There are two acres out back I could build on, but I doubt the owner would sell."

"Who owns them?" Ruth Rose asked.

"A man named Drake Turner," Carol said. "One of the richest men in Alaska. He uses the field to land his silly helicopter. You should hear the racket that thing makes!"

"We know him," Josh said. "Sort of. We're staying at his hotel. He owns a big yacht, too."

"Ah, yes," Carol said. "Mr. Turner owns a lot of things. I just wish he loved books as much as he loves his money!"

The kids thanked Carol and left.

"Let's check on the pool guys and their van," Dink said.

They hiked back to the harbor and stood behind some bushes.

The two pool guys were sitting in the shade. One was looking through a magazine. The other was sleeping with his shirt over his face.

"Okay, let's go back to the hotel," Dink said. "My dad will wonder what happened to us."

"And I wonder what we're having for dinner!" Josh added.

At eleven, the kids met in Ruth Rose's room. They all wore dark clothes. Ruth Rose stuck her camera in a pocket of her pants.

"What's that for?" Josh asked.

"If we see that baby orca getting kidnapped, a picture will prove it," Ruth Rose said.

They took the stairs down. Dink

peeked across the lobby. No Chester. They tiptoed closer. Then they heard squealing car tires and gunshots.

"Oh gosh, what's happening?" Josh said.

"That's just the TV," Ruth Rose whispered.

Chester was in his office, lying on the sofa with his shoes off. The TV was on, but his eyes were closed. He was snoring.

The kids crouched down and ran past the counter. Outside, it was dark. They raced toward the boat dock.

CHAPTER 9

The boat harbor was lit with lanterns on tall poles. There were more lights near the boats, making it seem almost like daytime.

"Why are there so many lights here?" Josh asked.

"I guess it's so the boat owners don't trip and fall in the water," Dink said.

They found the van where they had last seen it. The two pool men were standing near the dock, looking out to sea. One of them held a cell phone to his ear.

"I'd give anything to know what he's saying," Ruth Rose said quietly.

"We have to find a place to hide while we wait," Dink said.

"How about over there?" Josh asked. He pointed to a giant pine tree with lower branches that touched the ground. The branches created deep shadows.

"Perfect," Dink said. "We can watch the dock and the van from inside the branches, but no one can see us. Let's go!"

The kids ran over and crawled under the tree's bottom branches. Old pine needles covered the ground, making a soft place to sit.

"Cool, it's like being in a cave," Josh said. He made himself comfortable, leaning against the tree trunk.

Ruth Rose got out her camera.

Dink kept his eyes on the two men near the dock.

Minutes passed. Mosquitoes and other

tiny bugs flew around the kids' faces.

Josh closed his eyes. "Wake me when it gets exciting around here," he said.

Five minutes later Dink poked him. "Boat coming," he whispered.

Josh sat up. They all leaned forward, and Dink peeked between two branches. A boat the length of the *Jamaica* was pulling into an empty slip. A light shone on the deck, where three men were dragging a bulky tarp to the fore area of the boat.

"Look at that tarp," Ruth Rose whispered. "It's wiggling!"

The waiting pool men grabbed the front end of the boat, stopping it from hitting the dock pilings.

One of the men went to the van and backed it as close to the boat as possible. Then he jumped out and opened the rear doors.

The other pool guy and the men on the boat started laughing. Something

shiny was flopping around on the boat's deck. It was a large fish, and it wriggled its way into the water with a soft splash.

"Don't worry, mate," one of the men on the boat told the pool guy. "We got at least two hundred more of those for you."

"So are we even?" the pool guy asked.

"Yep, like we agreed," the guy on the boat said. "You give us a hundred bucks and new nets, we give you five hundred pounds of fresh salmon."

"Awesome!" the pool guy said, grabbing one end of the tarp. "Let's get these beauties into our van. We have to be there early if we want to get the best price at the markets."

Josh let out a sigh. *"Fish,"* he said. "The pool guys are here to buy fish, not a baby whale."

Ruth Rose dropped her camera back in her pocket.

The kids watched the men load the

salmon into the tank in their van. When they finished, they slammed the rear doors and drove away.

Feeling disappointed, Dink, Josh, and Ruth Rose walked toward the hotel. "Okay, so the pool guys didn't steal the baby orca," Dink said. "But *somebody* did, and the baby needs—"

Suddenly Josh put his hands out and stopped Dink and Ruth Rose. "Hide!" he said, and pulled them behind some bushes. They dropped to the ground.

"What are you doing?" Dink said.

"There's a guy walking right toward us!" Josh whispered. "Dink, I think it's your father!"

Dink sat up, peering along the walkway. The man was about the same height as his dad. He wore khaki pants, a blue shirt, and a baseball cap. He was carrying a gym bag with the letter *B* on the side.

"Not my dad," Dink whispered.

"That's a Boston Red Sox bag. Dad's a Yankees fan."

The stranger came closer, passing only a few feet away from the kids.

"It's Drake Turner!" Ruth Rose whispered.

Josh giggled nervously. "Maybe he wants to buy some *fish* for his pond!" he said.

Drake Turner kept walking, heading for the dock.

Dink waited five seconds, then stood up. "Come on," he said. "This is getting interesting!"

They followed Drake Turner, staying in the shadows. He moved quietly along the dock and seemed to be studying each boat. Finally, he stopped walking and let out a low whistle. After a few seconds, a light on one of the boats switched on. Drake hurried over and climbed aboard.

"What is he doing?" Josh whispered.

They were huddled behind a trash Dumpster.

"Getting on a boat," Dink said. "Talking to some guys. I can't hear what they're saying."

The kids left the shadow of the Dumpster and stepped onto the wooden dock.

"Look, there's Rafe's boat," Ruth Rose whispered. She pointed along the dock. The *Jamaica* rested in its slip, about ten boats away from the one Drake Turner had boarded. A yellow glow shone through one of the *Jamaica*'s portholes.

The kids approached the boat where Drake Turner and three men were talking. Twenty feet from the boat, Ruth Rose stopped short, and Josh ran into her.

"That's *NOT MY FALT*!" Ruth Rose exclaimed.

"No problem," Josh said. "It was *my* fault."

"No, the boat Drake Turner just got on is called *Not My Falt!*" Ruth Rose said. "That fishing boat we watched go out yesterday."

They crept closer until they were only ten feet from the boat. Hiding behind a tall wooden crate with FIRE HOSES printed on the side, they looked right onto the aft deck.

Four men stood on the deck, talking quietly. Drake Turner handed the gym bag to a man with muscled arms.

The man pulled open the zipper and looked inside.

CHAPTER 10

"Are you set to make the transfer early tomorrow morning?" Mr. Turner asked quietly.

The man with the gym bag nodded. "Before the sun comes up," he said. "Is the *Miranda* ready?"

"She's got a tank of water in the hold, like yours," he said.

"Where is she moored?" another man asked. He was taller than the others and had a bald head.

Drake Turner pointed over his shoulder. "Mooring number fifteen, right out there," he said. "The *Miranda* is too big to tie up here."

"We'll find her," the bald man said.

"Can I see the calf now?" Drake asked.

The other two men shoved a thick pile of nets to one side. One of them bent over and pulled open a trapdoor fitted into the deck. All four men looked down into the space. Drake Turner got on his knees and reached a hand into the opening.

The kids saw something wet move under Drake's hand. He stood up, nodded at the other men, and left the boat. The kids crouched as he passed their hiding place.

"It's Lily's baby!" Ruth Rose whispered.

Dink and Josh nodded.

They watched the men on the boat. On their hands and knees, the kids inched closer.

The man who had taken the gym bag stared down into the hold. He said something to the baby orca, then shook his head. "You know, I would never have done this if I didn't need the money," he told the other two men. "My wife is having her second surgery this week." He held up the gym bag. "I . . . I really need this money."

Suddenly Ruth Rose jumped up and raced straight toward the *Not My Falt.* She had her camera in her hand and snapped a picture.

When the flash went off, the men turned. One of them yelled, "HEY, YOU!"

Ruth Rose bolted down the wooden dock as fast as her legs would carry her. Behind her, she heard a voice yell, "It was some kid with a camera!"

Ruth Rose raced back to Dink and Josh. "Pine tree!" she called out as she shot past them.

Dink and Josh flew after Ruth Rose. Seconds later the boys dove through the tree's lower branches and threw themselves into the pine needles and dirt. Ruth Rose was already there. Dink felt his heart thumping hard in his chest. He thought he was going to faint.

The three men thundered past the tree. "Where the heck did the kid go?" one of them shouted. "We need that camera! Look everywhere!"

Josh was on his back, gulping mouthfuls of air. "I think I'm going to throw up," he gasped.

"You said you wanted excitement," Dink whispered.

"Yeah, the kind of excitement that gives me goose bumps," Josh said. "Not the kind that gives me a heart attack!"

"We can't stay here!" Ruth Rose whispered. "They'll come back and start searching!"

"All I want to do is go back to bed!" Josh said.

Ruth Rose was already crawling out from under the branches. "Rafe's boat!" she said as she sprinted toward the boat slips.

Dink and Josh raced after her onto the dock. This time they weren't trying to be quiet. Their sneakers pounded the wood planks as they ran.

In seconds they were standing next to the *Jamaica,* sweating and out of breath.

"Rafe!" Ruth Rose said. "Are you in there?"

Rafe Johnson's head popped out of his cabin door. "Ruth Rose?" he said. "What's going on, girl?"

"Can we come aboard?" Dink asked Rafe. "Some men are chasing us!"

Rafe grabbed Ruth Rose and pulled her onto the boat. Dink and Josh followed, and all of them clambered down into the cabin. Rafe slid the cabin door into place and threw a bolt.

"Now, what's going on?" he asked the three kids. "Who's chasing you?"

"The men who took the baby orca!" Ruth Rose said. "We found the calf!"

Rafe dimmed the lamp and turned off the TV. "Sit," he told the kids.

They squeezed together on a narrow sofa. Interrupting each other, they told Rafe how they had followed Drake Turner to the *Not My Falt.*

"He gave the guys on the boat a gym bag full of money!" Josh said.

"They're supposed to bring the calf to his yacht, the *Miranda,* tomorrow morning!" Dink added.

"The *Not My Falt* is Hector Falt's fishing boat," Rafe said. "I can't believe Hec would take a young orca away from its mother."

"We heard him say he really needs

the money," Dink said. "I guess his wife is sick."

Rafe nodded. "Some of us took up a collection to help pay her hospital bills," he said quietly. "I guess it wasn't enough."

"I saw Lily's baby," Ruth Rose said. She found the picture and handed the camera to Rafe.

"Wow, great shot," he said. "I see the calf's head. But you only got the men's legs. Without seeing their faces, we can't prove who was there."

"We know Mr. Turner was there," Ruth Rose said. "We all saw him hand over the money!"

"What about the calf?" Dink said. "How long can it go without Lily's milk?"

"A day or two," Rafe said.

"I think we should ask Mr. Turner to give the baby orca back to its mother," Ruth Rose said.

They all stared at her.

"But he just paid money for it!" Josh said. "He'd never return it."

"He might," Ruth Rose said. "But if he won't, we can call the police."

Dink nodded. "Let's go try," he said.

Ruth Rose asked Rafe to bring his tape recorder and the tape of Naomi's cries.

The four of them left the *Jamaica* and hurried toward the Turner Hotel.

"I bet he won't even talk to us," Josh said.

The kids and Rafe trooped into the hotel lobby. Chester was still snoring in his office as they headed for the elevator.

"Can I push the button, please?" Josh asked once they were all inside.

"Go for it," Dink said.

Josh mashed the button with the big 4-P on it. The elevator hummed as it took them to Drake Turner's penthouse. When the elevator door opened, they stepped into a small carpeted room. There was a chair, a mirror on the wall, and a vase of flowers. Next to the flowers was a door with a peephole.

Dink leaned his ear against the door. "I think I hear a TV," he said.

Ruth Rose looked at Rafe. He set the tape recorder outside Drake Turner's door and inserted the tape. "Ready," he said.

Ruth Rose knocked on the door. Nothing happened. She knocked again, louder.

"I think the TV went off," Dink whispered.

"Who's out there?" a voice asked through the door.

"Ruth Rose and Dink and Josh," Ruth Rose said. "We're staying in your hotel."

"What do you want?" the voice asked. "It's late."

"We want you to listen to something," Ruth Rose said. She nodded at Rafe, who switched on the tape recorder. The hallway was suddenly filled with whale cries. Naomi was grieving for her lost baby.

CHAPTER 11

A minute later the door opened. Drake Turner stood there. His eyes were red. "What's that?" he asked, pointing at the recorder.

"Orca cries," Rafe said. "It's a mother orca whose baby died."

Mr. Turner listened to the awful sounds. When the tape ran out, the hallway was quiet. "Who are you?" he asked Rafe.

"Rafe Johnson. I own the *Jamaica,* one of the whale-watching boats," Rafe said. "I keep a slip near the *Not My Falt.*"

Ruth Rose showed Mr. Turner her camera. "I took a picture of you and those guys on the boat," she said. "And the baby orca you stole."

Drake Turner backed away from the door. "I . . . I have nothing to say," he muttered.

"Could we talk to you?" Dink asked. "It's important!"

"The baby whale could die!" Josh said. "It needs milk from its mother!" Josh picked up the tape recorder. "That baby whale you took has a mother, and she's crying, too."

Drake Turner stared at the floor. Then he nodded. "Please come in," he said.

All the lights were on in the apartment. The carpet was thick and white. The furniture was black leather. The gray walls were hung with photos of Mr. Turner with a smiling redheaded woman and a redheaded boy. The pictures showed them at the beach, aboard the *Miranda*, and in front of a Christmas tree.

"This way," Drake Turner said. He led them down a hallway and stopped in front of a closed door.

He let out a big sigh. "My wife took my son away from me a year ago," he said. His voice was shaky. "I . . . miss them terribly. I've tried everything to get them back, searched everywhere, but nothing came of it."

He glanced at Josh. "Tyler has hair the same color as yours," he said, opening the door and switching on a light. It was a little boy's room. A mural of whales swimming in the ocean had been painted on one wall. A bulletin board held pictures of whales. A whale mobile hung from the ceiling, and a stuffed whale lay on the little bed.

"Tyler loves whales, as you can see," Drake Turner said. He pointed to a little kid's crayon drawing of a whale. "The night Miranda and Tyler left, I found that on my desk. I don't know why he colored it green."

He sat on Tyler's bed. He picked up the stuffed whale and held it on his lap. "I know I've been stupid, but I was desperate. Tyler's birthday is next week. The baby orca is for him, if I ever find him. I . . . know I broke the law. But Tyler's not coming back, so it was all for nothing," he said.

"But how would you even keep a baby orca alive?" Rafe asked. "The young ones need their mothers for at least a year. They need saltwater. They need their orca families."

"At my place down the coast, I built a special pond," Mr. Turner said. "It's an inlet of the ocean, and I dammed it

up to form a sort of outdoor aquarium. I hired a whale expert to help take care of it. The calf would have everything it needs."

"But that pond would be like a prison to an orca," Rafe said. "It needs its mother and her milk. Orcas live in family pods. The baby would be miserable alone in a pond. It would probably die within six months."

"We came to ask you to return the baby to its mother," Ruth Rose said. "Please."

"There's still time, Mr. Turner," Rafe said.

Drake Turner stroked the stuffed whale, then set it on Tyler's pillow. "Of course I will," he said. "I never thought about the mother's milk. I never meant to cause it any harm. I just wanted my family back."

Everyone got quiet.

The sad man stood up. "I'll go talk to Hec Falt," he said. "I'll persuade him to release the little orca as soon as possible."

"Thank you!" Ruth Rose cried.

Josh was studying the drawing of the green whale. He looked at Mr. Turner. "Do you have a computer?" he asked.

"Of course, but why . . . ?"

"I think I know where your son might be," Josh said. "I can show you on a computer."

Drake Turner hurried from the room and returned with his laptop. He booted it up and handed it to Josh.

Josh found a search engine, typed in a few words, then waited while something came up on the screen. "Do you know that book Tyler was so crazy about?" he asked.

Drake Turner shook his head. "I'm afraid I never took the time to read with him," he said. "I don't know what books Tyler was reading."

"He loved a book called *Wonderful Island,*" Dink said.

"He got everyone in the hotel to read it to him," Ruth Rose said.

Josh pointed to Tyler's green whale drawing. "That's not a green whale," he told Mr. Turner. "That's a picture of the island that Jamie went to with his parents in the book. The island is shaped like a whale. Tyler copied it when he made the drawing."

Josh showed the picture on the laptop screen. It was a photo of Frye Island, taken from the air.

"It *does* look like Tyler's drawing," Drake Turner said.

Josh handed the laptop to Mr. Turner. "I think your wife took Tyler to Frye Island," he said. "I'll bet Tyler drew the island and left the picture on your desk as a clue. I'll bet anything he *wants* you to go there and find him."

Mr. Turner studied the laptop screen and Tyler's green drawing. "This Frye Island really exists?" he said.

"It's in Sebago Lake, in Maine," Ruth Rose said. "We read the book in the library today."

"Why would Tyler's mother take him

to Maine?" Drake Turner asked. "She's never been there. She used to go to Europe, so I've had the detectives search Paris and Rome and the other big cities. Miranda would never take our son to some little island in the middle of nowhere."

"Maybe Tyler wants to do all the things the boy in the story did," Ruth Rose said. "He could have talked his mom into taking him there. Plus, she knew you'd never think of looking for them in Maine."

Mr. Turner pulled a cell phone from his pocket. He tapped in a number, then said, "Mr. Cosgrove? This is Drake Turner.... Yes, I know it's after midnight. I'm sorry if I woke you. I need you to have your detectives check out Frye Island. It's in Sebago Lake, in Maine. Yes, Maine. Check the hotels and bed-and-breakfasts. There's a chance that my wife and son are there."

Mr. Turner listened. "Thank you, Mr. Cosgrove. This means everything to me."

He hung up. "Now let's see if Hec Falt answers *his* phone in the middle of the night!"

Then he tapped in another number. "Mr. Falt?" he said. "This is Drake Turner. I'm calling to ask for a special favor from you."

He handed the phone to Rafe. "Please explain to Mr. Falt how he should release the baby whale," he said.

CHAPTER 12

Rafe stepped into the hallway with the phone.

Dink pulled out his own cell phone and called his father. First he explained why he wasn't asleep in his room. Then he told his dad they had found the baby orca. "We're all going to release it right now!" he said. "Meet us in the lobby!"

Ten minutes later Mr. Turner, Rafe, and the kids took the elevator to the lobby. Dink's father was there. His eyes looked sleepy, but he was smiling. "Every time

I take my eyes off you kids, you get involved in some mystery!" he said.

He and Rafe and Mr. Turner all shook hands. It was after one in the morning.

Suddenly Chester popped his head out of his office. His hair was standing up, and his shirt was wrinkled. "What's going on?" he asked. "Is the hotel on fire?"

Drake Turner laughed. "No, Chester. You can go back to sleep," he said. "We're going to the docks."

"Fishing?" Chester asked, rubbing his eyes.

"No, Operation Orca!" Mr. Turner said.

Hec Falt had sent his crew home. So it was just Hec, Rafe, Mr. Turner, Dink's father, and the three kids aboard the *Not My Falt* when it headed out to sea. The sea and sky were dark, with only a few stars reflecting on the water.

While Hec steered the boat, Rafe stood next to him and they talked quietly. After a few minutes, Rafe motioned for Mr. Turner to join him and Hec. Then Hec handed Mr. Turner the gym bag with the *B* on its side. All three men shook hands.

Rafe walked over to the kids and Dink's father. "Mr. Turner apologized to Hec for involving him in this orca capture," Rafe said. "They're both going to turn themselves in to the authorities tomorrow. Hec feels terrible about taking the baby, and he's anxious to return it to its mother."

Mr. Turner left Hec and joined the others. He set the gym bag on the boat deck.

Dink remembered the briefcase. "Mr. Turner, did you give some guy your briefcase yesterday? One with your initials on the side?" he asked. "He has a van with *Cool Pool Brothers* on it."

"I think you mean Dennis Toomey," Drake Turner said. "He and Chester are brothers. They own the pool business together."

"I thought Dennis Toomey looked familiar," Dink said. "He looks like his brother!"

"We think he gave Chester some money yesterday," Ruth Rose said. "We thought the Cool Pool guys were the ones who took the baby whale. We thought it was your briefcase because it had *D.T.* on it."

"I don't own a briefcase with my initials on it," Mr. Turner said. "And I believe Dennis gives Chester money to put in the safe now and then. Money from their pool business."

"So *D.T.* stands for *Dennis Toomey*," Josh said. "Cool!"

Just then Mr. Turner's cell phone chirped in his pocket. He tapped a key and said, "Hello, this is Drake."

He listened, then closed his eyes. "Your men found them?" he asked. "Yes, red hair, both of them. Great work, Mr. Cosgrove. Let's talk in the morning. I'm in the middle of something important. Thank you very, very much!"

Mr. Turner was beaming. "Miranda and Tyler are renting a cottage on Frye Island," he said. "She's had to explain to Tyler that there are no whales in Sebago Lake."

"Awesome!" Josh said. "Are you going there?"

"I'll fly in as soon as I can," he said. "I don't know what Miranda will say, but I have to try. I know I can be a better husband and father." His eyes looked hopeful. "How can I thank you?"

"Josh is dying to see your yacht!" Dink said.

Drake smiled at Josh. "Really? You'd like to come aboard the *Miranda*?"

"Sure!" Josh said. "Only I'm too polite to ask you. Dink isn't polite at all!"

Mr. Turner laughed. "Let's have lunch on the *Miranda* tomorrow," he said. "I'll send the dinghy to the dock at noon. But lunch doesn't seem nearly enough. I'd like to do something special for you kids."

"I know something," Dink said. "We met a lady—"

Before Dink could continue, they all felt Hec slow his boat. "Here, Rafe?" Hec asked. "How can you tell in the middle of the night?"

"I've been to this spot a thousand times," Rafe said, looking out at the dark sea through his binoculars.

Hec flipped on a searchlight and

aimed it onto the water, sweeping it back and forth in a slow arc. No one saw a fin or any signs of whales breathing.

"Can we try a different spot?" Rafe asked Hec after a minute. He pointed. "A few hundred yards to the right."

"Sure." The *Not My Falt* moved slowly to the new location. The searchlight continued to cast a beam on the dark water.

"I see something!" Dink cried. "Or I think I did!"

Hec turned the light to where Dink was pointing.

"Yes!" Rafe said. "It's a pod, all right. Closer, Hec?"

Hec guided the boat toward the pod. "Fins!" he cried.

Rafe trained his binoculars on one fin that was six feet out of the water. "That's Jack!" he said. "You found the pod, Hec!"

"Okay, let's do it," Hec said to Rafe. He slowed the boat, then walked over to the machine with the crane arm that could be swung, raised, and lowered. A large hook hung from its dangling cable. Using a lever, Hec guided the arm to a spot over the trapdoor.

Hec and Rafe pulled the trapdoor lid, and everyone looked down into the hold. The young orca was lying still in several inches of water. Its blowhole made little chuffing sounds as the calf breathed in and out.

"I've been talking to the baby, keeping it calm," Hec told Rafe. "Do you think it understood me?"

"Sure," Rafe said. "Orcas are very smart."

"We poured in cold seawater every hour," Hec added.

"You did well," Rafe said. He looked at the calf. "Time to go see your mama, little one."

CHAPTER 13

"The calf's lying on a canvas stretcher inside the tank," Hec said. "I'll hook the crane to the stretcher to lift it out. Then, if you'll all guide it, we'll take it over to the side."

Hec pulled the big steel hook lower. A strap was woven through slots along the edges of the stretcher. He slipped the hook under the strap.

"Now, as the crane lifts, you guys all grab on and keep the stretcher even," Hec said.

"Are you sure this will work?" Rafe asked.

Hec nodded. "This is how I haul in nets filled with fish," he said. "It's how I brought the calf aboard last night."

He pulled the lever, and the crane cable became taut. Slowly, the stretcher

began to rise out of the tank. Water
dripped on everyone as they held on to
keep the load from tipping or swinging.

"Keep it even!" Hec cried. "Don't let
the baby slip out!"

The crane arm moved to the side
of the boat. Six pairs of hands held on

to the stretcher. The calf wriggled and thumped its tail. Dink heard it make little crying noises.

"Just a few more seconds," Dink whispered.

"Okay, I'm going to lower it to the water," Hec said. "Watch your hands! Don't get pinched!"

The crane arm moved the stretcher out over the water, and Hec lowered it.

They all watched as the baby orca sank into the water. The calf lay still for a minute, then wriggled free from the stretcher. It floated on the surface, blowing air through its blowhole.

Suddenly a tall, curved fin appeared from below the calf. Air blew from a blowhole, making a small jet next to the baby.

"It's Lily!" Dink cried.

"Now, this is what I call exciting!" Josh said.

Lily nuzzled her baby, bumping it gently with her nose.

The baby went immediately to Lily's side for milk. Lily dove, and the baby followed.

"Well, that was something special," Hec muttered. He used the lever to get the crane arm and stretcher back aboard his boat.

Mr. Turner clapped. "Well done, Hector!" he said.

Dink tried to say something, but he had a lump in his throat.

His father had tears in his eyes.

"Rats!" Ruth Rose said. "I was so excited, I forgot to take pictures!"

At noon the next day, Dink, Josh, and Ruth Rose were waiting on the dock.

A white rubber dinghy sped across the water toward them. It slowed and came to rest against one of the pilings.

"I'm Simon from the *Miranda*," the pilot said. "Are you kids Mr. Turner's luncheon guests?"

"Yes!" Josh said.

Simon helped the kids step down from the dock to the dinghy. It moved under their feet. "Is this really made of rubber?" Josh asked.

"Very strong rubber," Simon said. He handed out three life vests. "Strap these on, please."

A minute later they were racing across the water. Salt spray flew up and wet their faces. Their hair flew back, and their eyes watered.

Dink saw the *Miranda* in the distance. As they came alongside, he realized the boat seemed bigger than 120 feet.

"Welcome aboard!" Drake Turner shouted down from the upper deck. The dinghy rested against a ladder, and

Simon helped each kid put a foot on the bottom rung.

On the deck, a crew member took their life vests and handed them towels to dry their hair and faces.

"Simon loves to speed that dinghy," Drake Turner said. "He likes to see how wet he can get my guests."

Another crew member stood behind Mr. Turner. He held a tray carrying three tall glasses of orange juice.

"Follow me," Mr. Turner said as the kids sipped their juice. "Lunch is almost ready."

He brought them to a table standing in the shade of an awning. The table was set with a white tablecloth and blue plates.

"I hope you like burgers and fries and ice cream," Drake Turner said. "That was the chef's suggestion."

"Tell the chef we love him!" Josh called out.

The crew member who had served the orange juice arrived with a covered platter. He removed the top and set the platter on a tray stand next to the table.

When everyone had a burger and plenty of fries, Drake Turner said, "Last night, seeing the mother orca reunited with her baby, I realized how foolish I was, taking the baby. I want to thank you for making me see that what I did was wrong."

Mr. Turner took a sip of his water. "Now, on the boat you started to tell me about a lady?" he said.

"Her name is Carol Waxman," Dink said. "She's a librarian in town."

"Oh yes," Mr. Turner said. "I own the piece of land behind the library. My pilot puts the helicopter there now and then."

"Well, she has a problem," Ruth Rose said.

The kids explained how tiny the library was, with not nearly enough room for all the books. They told him how Carol wanted to buy the land so she could expand the library.

"She can't do it because she doesn't have enough money," Josh said.

Drake Turner stared out to sea for a minute, then called to one of his crew members. "Ronnie, bring my phone, will you, please?"

Ronnie brought a silver smartphone to the table.

"Can you get me the number for Carol Waxman?" Mr. Turner said. "She's a librarian."

Ronnie tapped a few keys, then dialed a number. "Hold on, please," he said, then handed the phone to his boss.

"Hello, is this Ms. Waxman?" he asked. "This is Drake Turner speaking. I land my helicopter behind your library."

He winked at the kids. "I know the helicopter is noisy and smelly, Ms. Waxman. Starting now, that land belongs to your library," he told her. "No more helicopters in your backyard. I'll send the paperwork tomorrow."

The kids could hear Carol's excited "Thank you!" over the phone.

"Don't thank me," he said. "Thank those three kids who came in to see you yesterday, the ones from Connecticut."

More thankful sounds came from Mr. Turner's cell phone.

"One more thing, Ms. Waxman," Drake Turner said. "I want to help you build an extension to the library. I'll bring a check to you tomorrow, and I have friends who will also donate."

They all heard Carol Waxman's joy over the phone.

Josh and Ruth Rose were beaming.

Dink put down his hamburger. He

couldn't swallow, and he was blinking back tears.

Drake Turner handed the cell phone back to Ronnie. "I'll be taking the chopper to the airport tomorrow, Ronnie," he said. "Will you ask the pilot to pick me up behind the library . . . for the last time?"

Drake looked at the kids. "Carol Waxman says she owes you each a big hug," he said.

Josh giggled.

Mr. Turner set his napkin down. "Well, this has been an expensive lunch!" he said, pretending to be angry.

"Are we done?" Josh asked, looking panicked. "I thought there was ice cream!"

DID YOU FIND THE
SECRET MESSAGE
HIDDEN IN THIS BOOK?

If you *don't* want
to know the answer,
don't look at the bottom
of this page!

HAVE YOU READ ALL THE BOOKS IN THE

A to Z Mysteries®

SERIES?

Help Dink, Josh, and Ruth Rose . . .

...solve
mysteries
from A to Z!

Collect clues with
Dink, Josh, and Ruth Rose
in their next exciting
adventure

SECRET
ADMIRER

"Who wants a secret admirer who can't
even spell *secret*?"

Josh grinned at Dink. "Someone liiiiikes
you!" he teased.

Dink stared at Josh. "Did *you* leave the
note?" he demanded. "If you did, I'll . . ."

Josh shook his head. "Nope. Not me,"
he said. "Maybe it was Ruth Rose!"

"Ha!" Ruth Rose said. "I'm a good
speller, Joshua!"

Dink stared out the window at the fall-
ing snowflakes. "Then who could it be?"

A to Z Mysteries® fans, check out Ron Roy's other great mystery series!

Capital Mysteries

#1: Who Cloned the President?
#2: Kidnapped at the Capital
#3: The Skeleton in the Smithsonian
#4: A Spy in the White House
#5: Who Broke Lincoln's Thumb?
#6: Fireworks at the FBI
#7: Trouble at the Treasury
#8: Mystery at the Washington Monument
#9: A Thief at the National Zoo
#10: The Election-Day Disaster
#11: The Secret at Jefferson's Mansion
#12: The Ghost at Camp David
#13: Trapped on the D.C. Train!
#14: Turkey Trouble on the National Mall

Calendar Mysteries

January Joker
February Friend
March Mischief
April Adventure
May Magic
June Jam
July Jitters
August Acrobat
September Sneakers
October Ogre
November Night
December Dog
New Year's Eve Thieves

If Josh makes you laugh, meet another funny redhead!

MARVIN REDPOST

LOUIS SACHAR
Winner of the Newbery Medal for Holes
MARVIN REDPOST
Why Pick on Me?

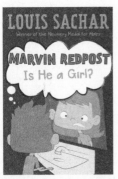

LOUIS SACHAR
Winner of the Newbery Medal for Holes
MARVIN REDPOST
Is He a Girl?

LOUIS SACHAR
Winner of the Newbery Medal for Holes
MARVIN REDPOST
Alone in His Teacher's House

LOUIS SACHAR
Winner of the Newbery Medal for Holes
MARVIN REDPOST
Class President

LOUIS SACHAR
Winner of the Newbery Medal for Holes
MARVIN REDPOST
A Flying Birthday Cake?

LOUIS SACHAR
Winner of the Newbery Medal for Holes
MARVIN REDPOST
Kidnapped at Birth?

LOUIS SACHAR
Winner of the Newbery Medal for Holes
MARVIN REDPOST
Super Fast, Out of Control!

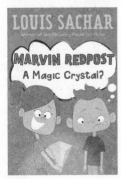

LOUIS SACHAR
Winner of the Newbery Medal for Holes
MARVIN REDPOST
A Magic Crystal?

If you like **A TO Z MYSTERIES**®, take a swing at

BALLPARK® Mysteries

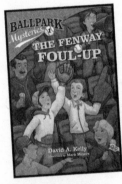